GEORGE W. BUSH'S 9/11 ADDRESS TO THE NATION

FRONT SEAT OF HISTORY: FAMOUS SPEECHES

TAMRA ORR

CHERRY LAKE PRESS

Published in the United States of America by Cherry Lake Publishing Group
Ann Arbor, Michigan
www.cherrylakepublishing.com

Reading Adviser: Marla Conn, MS, Ed., Literacy specialist, Read-Ability, Inc.
Content Adviser: Adam Fulton Johnson, PhD, Assistant Professor, History, Philosophy, and Sociology of Science, Michigan State University
Photo credits: © The U.S. National Archives, P7376-22, cover; © The U.S. National Archives, P7060-19A, 5; © The U.S. National Archives, P7091-18, 6; ©The U.S. National Archives, P7475-05A, 8; ©The U.S. National Archives, P7492-06, 9; ©The U.S. National Archives, P7680-23, 10; © Library of Congress, LC-DIG-ppmsca-01932, 13; © The U.S. National Archives, P7803-03A, 14; © The U.S. National Archives, P8999-11A, 16; © The U.S. National Archives, P7377-02, 19; © The U.S. National Archives, P7365-23A, 20; © The U.S. National Archives, P9154-30, 23; © Glynnis Jones/Shutterstock.com, 24; © Christopher Penler/Shutterstock.com, 25, 29 [top]; © BrandonKleinVideo/Shutterstock.com, 26; © Joseph Sohm/Shutterstock.com, 28; © The U.S. National Archives, P7784-32, 29 [bottom]

Cherry Lake Press is an imprint of Cherry Lake Publishing Group.

Library of Congress Cataloging-in-Publication Data
Names: Orr, Tamra, author.
Title: George W. Bush's 9/11 address to the nation / by Tamra Orr.
Description: Ann Arbor, Michigan : Cherry Lake Publishing, 2021 | Series: Front seat of history: famous speeches | Includes bibliographical references and index. | Audience: Grades 4-6.
Identifiers: LCCN 2020005542 (print) | LCCN 2020005543 (ebook) | ISBN 9781534168824 (hardcover) | ISBN 9781534170506 (paperback) | ISBN 9781534172340 (pdf) | ISBN 9781534174184 (ebook)
Subjects: LCSH: September 11 Terrorist Attacks, 2001—Juvenile literature. | Bush, George W. (George Walker), 1946—Juvenile literature. | Speeches, addresses, etc., American—Juvenile literature. | Presidents—United States—Messages—Juvenile literature.
Classification: LCC HV6432.7 .O789 2021 (print) | LCC HV6432.7 (ebook) | DDC 973.931—dc23
LC record available at https://lccn.loc.gov/2020005542
LC ebook record available at https://lccn.loc.gov/2020005543

Cherry Lake Publishing Group would like to acknowledge the work of the Partnership for 21st Century Learning, a Network of Battelle for Kids. Please visit http://www.battelleforkids.org/networks/p21 for more information.

Printed in the United States of America
Corporate Graphics

ABOUT THE AUTHOR

Tamra Orr is the author of more than 500 nonfiction books for readers of all ages. A graduate of Ball State University, she now lives in the Pacific Northwest with her family. When she isn't writing books, she is either camping, reading or on the computer researching the latest topics.

TABLE OF CONTENTS

An Unforgettable Moment

In the early morning hours of September 11, 2001, the United States was attacked. In less than 90 minutes, four planes had crashed, more than 3,000 people had died, and the country was in shock. The attack came from the **terrorist** group al-Qaeda, led by a man named Osama bin Laden. The people of the United States looked to their president for words of comfort and reassurance. George W. Bush had only been in office for 8 months when this tragedy struck America. When he addressed the nation on the night of 9/11, the entire world was listening.

[21ST CENTURY SKILLS LIBRARY]

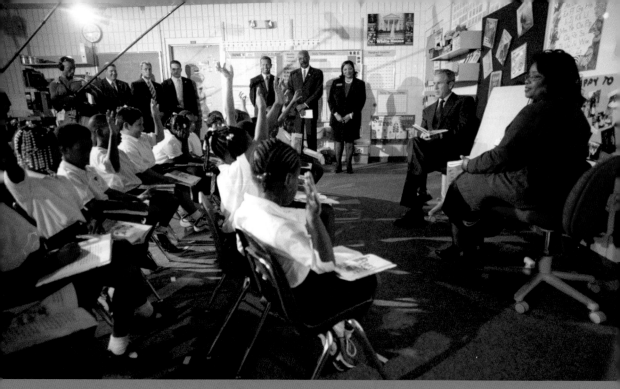

President Bush was visiting a classroom in Sarasota, Florida, when he received news of the first attack.

Grand Rapids, Michigan. 8:55 am. Cassidy sat on the couch and fiddled with her school uniform. She had a dentist appointment scheduled for this morning, so she would be arriving late to school. This would have been fun, but her mom still made her dress in her uniform. She decided to flip on the TV while she waited for her

On his way back to Washington, DC, President Bush speaks on the phone with Vice President Dick Cheney.

mom to finish feeding her brother Teddy breakfast. The TV was set to the news channel, and the image on the screen made her pause. The video was live from New York City. The text below the screen read: Breaking News: World Trade Center Disaster.

"Mom!" shouted Cassidy. "Mom, get in here!"

Mrs. Cooper hurried in from the kitchen with Teddy on her hip. "What in the world are you yelling . . ." her voice faded away quickly as she stared at the TV. She sat down on the end of the couch and reached for her daughter's hand. The two watched in horror as smoke billowed out from the North Twin Tower.

"Was it an accident?" whispered Cassidy. Mrs. Cooper was silent and shocked, tears already streaming down her face. Seconds later, the answer became clear as a second plane came into sight and struck the South Tower. Cassidy covered her eyes, and Mrs. Cooper put her arm around her shoulders. "Go and stay in your room with your brother. I'll get you when it's time to leave" she said, handing Teddy to her. "He's too young to see any of this."

Cassidy gratefully left the living room. She found it hard to process what she had just seen. It seemed like one of the disaster movies she and her dad watched together on the weekends. Only this time it was real, with actual people inside of those planes and buildings. She shuddered at the thought.

First Lady Laura Bush welcomes servicemen at a memorial service for United Flight 93.

That night, after Teddy had gone to bed, Cassidy's parents explained exactly what had happened. Four airplanes had been **hijacked** by 19 terrorists from the group known as al-Qaeda. Two of the airplanes had been sent to the Twin Towers in New York City, while another had hit the **Pentagon** in Washington, DC.

"What about the fourth?" she asked, not sure if she really wanted to know the answer.

President Bush and White House staff share a moment of silence.

People wave flags as President Bush departs the White House.

"The passengers on that plane were able to regain control, so it didn't reach its target," Mr. Cooper replied carefully. "But their plane crashed in a field in Pennsylvania. They lost their lives."

"How many people died today?" Cassidy asked, but this time she was sure she didn't want to hear the answer.

"Almost 3,000, including more than 400 **first responders**," Mrs. Cooper said, wiping tears from her face. She reached for her daughter's hand. "The president is about to speak to the nation about what happened."

As they sat down in front of the living room TV, Cassidy tried to imagine being the president at a time like this. She had no idea what President George W. Bush could possibly say. But she knew that whatever it was, this was a moment she would never, ever forget—even if she wanted to.

The World Reacts

Across the globe, many nations reacted to al-Qaeda's attack on America with horror and sympathy. The French newspaper Le Monde *wrote, "Today, we are all Americans." In England, "The Star-Spangled Banner" played during Buckingham Palace's changing of the guard. In Rio de Janeiro, billboards were put up that showed Brazil's famous Christ the Redeemer statue hugging the New York City skyline. In other countries, there were moments of silence in their streets, on television, over the radio, and in schools. Flags were flown at half-mast. Other nations held candlelight* **vigils***, knelt in prayer, signed letters of sympathy, and sent medical supplies. Firefighters around the world put ribbons on their trucks, and in Poland they sounded their sirens all at once.*

"The Brightest Beacon"

The only sound in the Coopers' living room was President George W. Bush's voice and the occasional sniffle from Mrs. Cooper. The president sat at a desk in the White House, his hands clasped in front of him.

"Today, our fellow citizens, our way of life, our very freedom came under attack in a series of deliberate and deadly terrorist acts," he stated. "The victims were in airplanes or in their offices: secretaries, business men and women, military and federal workers, moms and dads, friends and neighbors."

Cassidy wondered if any of the kids from her school would be affected by the tragedy. Had they lost someone they knew?

[21ST CENTURY SKILLS LIBRARY]

Three nuns view a wall with missing person notices after the 9/11 attacks.

First Lady Laura Bush and others place flowers at a memorial honoring the firefighters who lost their lives.

"Thousands of lives were suddenly ended by evil, **despicable** acts of terror," President Bush continued. "The pictures of airplanes flying into buildings, fires burning, huge structures collapsing have filled us with disbelief, terrible sadness, and a quiet, unyielding anger. These acts of mass murder were intended to frighten our nation into chaos and retreat. But they have failed. Our country is strong."

"I don't feel strong," whispered Mrs. Cooper. Cassidy knew just how her mother felt.

The president continued, "A great people has been moved to defend a great nation. Terrorist attacks can shake the foundations of our biggest buildings, but they cannot touch the foundation of America. These acts shatter steel, but they cannot dent the steel of American **resolve**. America was targeted for attack because we're the brightest beacon for freedom and opportunity in the world. And no one will keep that light from shining. Today, our nation saw evil—the very worst of human nature—and we responded with the best of America. With the daring of our rescue workers, with the caring for strangers and neighbors who came to give blood and help in any way they could."

"I'm going to donate blood first thing tomorrow morning," said Mr. Cooper.

President Bush signs the Patriot Act in October 2001. Its purpose is to help the U.S. government detect terrorism quickly.

"Isn't Dad afraid of needles?" Cassidy whispered to her mother.

"Yes, but this is his way of doing something," she replied. "We feel like we should be helping in some way."

Next, the president informed the American people that he had put the government's emergency response plan into action. "Our first priority is to get help to those who have been injured and to take every precaution to protect our citizens at home and around the world from further attacks," he said. He explained that, despite the attacks, federal agencies would be open for business again in the morning. He also reassured listeners that the country's economy remained strong.

Although Cassidy felt better, she knew that the country would be recovering from this assault for more than just days or weeks. She suspected it would take years.

Coloring a Threat

After 9/11, the American government wanted to make sure that it could better protect the country from any terrorist attacks in the future. In October of that year, **legislation** was introduced to create the Department of Homeland Security. In June 2002, the department was approved. Part of its responsibility was creating a Homeland Security Advisory System. This system had color-coded threat alerts, from low (green) to high (red). It was a quick and simple way to let Americans know if there was a current threat and, if there was, the seriousness of it.

"All That Is Good and Just"

Back on the couch, Mr. Cooper put his arm around Cassidy and his wife. Together, the three of them listened to the rest of the president's speech.

"The search is underway for those who were behind these evil acts," the president said. He made it clear that the country would "make no distinction" between the terrorists and anyone who protected them. "America and our friends and allies join with all those who want peace and security in the world, and we stand together to win the war against terrorism," he stated.

"Are we at war?" Cassidy asked, confused.

"Hmm, we may be," said Mr. Cooper. "I've never heard of a war on terrorism, though."

Firefighters gather around President George W. Bush
as he visits the site of the World Trade Center.

"How can we fight an idea rather than people?" Mrs. Cooper
wondered aloud.

Cassidy could tell that the president's speech was almost over
when he paused to ask for prayers for those people "whose sense
of safety and security has been threatened." He finished by saying,
"This is a day when all Americans from every walk of life unite in
our resolve for justice and peace. America has stood down enemies
before, and we will do so this time. None of us will ever forget this

President Bush's speech to firefighters was not planned.

day, yet we go forward to defend freedom and all that is good and just in our world. Good night. And God bless America."

The Coopers turned off the television. Turning off the TV felt wrong, but continuing to watch the videos from the attacks was too horrifying. The house felt especially quiet that night.

In the following days, the people of New York City walked around in a daze. School was canceled. Candlelight vigils were held. Wherever Cassidy looked, she saw American flags. They flew on people's porches and balconies.

"I Can Hear You!"

Three days after the attacks, President Bush traveled to what became known as "ground zero." This was the spot in New York City where the Twin Towers had once been. At one point, he climbed up a pile of rubble and stood next to a firefighter. He grabbed a bullhorn and began thanking first responders. When someone in the crowd yelled that they could not hear him, Bush shouted back words that would go down in history. "I can hear you!" he yelled. "The rest of the world hears you! And the people—and the people who knocked these buildings down will hear all of us soon!" The crowd's reaction was instantaneous. They began screaming, "USA! USA!" It was a moment that showed the country's bravery, determination, and resolve.

Remembering Those Lost

Cassidy took a deep breath. Her family was visiting New York City for the weekend. It had been 10 years since the 9/11 attacks, but she still felt uneasy about visiting the site of the Twin Towers. She could still see the images that had flashed on every television. They had given her nightmares.

But she was here. Teddy stood beside her, now a full head taller than her. He was the same age she had been when the attacks happened. The Twin Towers were long gone, but in their place was one of the most visited spots in New York—the 9/11 Memorial.

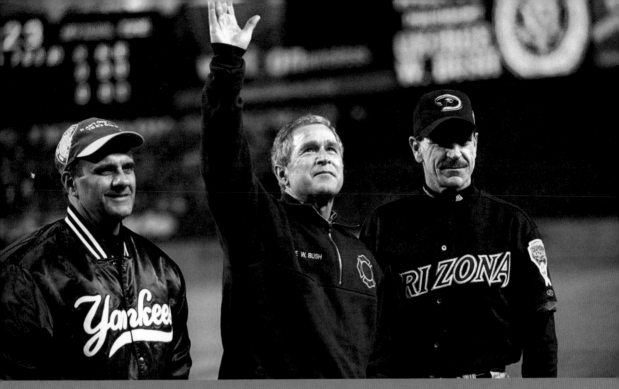

President George W. Bush threw the first pitch in Yankee Stadium in New York during the World Series in 2001.

There were two man-made waterfalls, their water plunging down and out of sight. Both had been built where the towers' foundations had originally been.

Teddy looked over at the low bronze walls surrounding the pool. "Oh wow, Cass," he said softly. "Do you see all of these names?"

There are 3,000 names inscribed on the 9/11 memorial.

Cassidy looked at the thousands of names engraved on the walls. She gently ran her fingers over the letters. "It includes the first responders," she replied. The two stood there quietly, feeling the loss of so many people. Their mother and father came up behind them.

"Let's go and see the Survivor Tree," Mrs. Cooper suggested, placing a hand on Cassidy's shoulder.

The Survivor Tree stands next to One World Trade Center, also called the Freedom Tower, which opened in 2014.

Michael Arad, the architect for the memorial, said
the pools represent "absence made visible."

"What's that?" Teddy asked.

"It's the pear tree that recovery workers found at ground zero,"
Mr. Cooper replied. "The New York City Parks and Recreation
Department worked to keep it alive. When it was strong enough,
it was planted here. It's the perfect symbol of America's strength
and determination."

"That sounds good," Teddy said.

Cassidy smiled sadly. It was good. She thought back to President Bush's words 10 years earlier. As he had predicted, she had never forgotten that day. She just hoped she could keep focusing on everything that was "good and just" in the world. For now, that meant it was time for her and her family to get some lunch and enjoy New York City in the summertime.

Closure at Last

Despite continuing efforts, it took until May 2011 for Osama bin Laden to be found and killed. The raid in Abbottabad, Pakistan, was carried out by U.S. Special Forces, under orders from President Barack Obama. Bin Laden's body was buried soon after in the Arabian Sea off the deck of the USS Carl Vinson. Obama spoke that night from the White House. "Finally," he stated, "let me say to the families who lost loved ones on 9/11 that we have never forgotten your loss, nor wavered in our commitment to see that we do whatever it takes to prevent another attack on our shores."

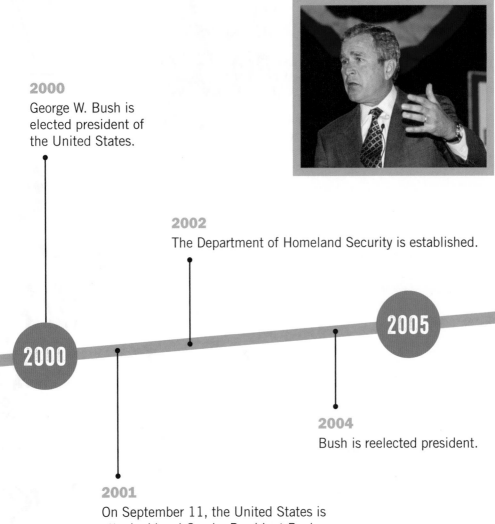

2000

George W. Bush is elected president of the United States.

2002

The Department of Homeland Security is established.

2005

2000

2004

Bush is reelected president.

2001

On September 11, the United States is attacked by al-Qaeda; President Bush establishes Operation Enduring Freedom, which starts the war in Afghanistan.